Wish You Were Here

Anushka Ravishankar

Illustrated by Various Artists

SWEET HOME HOME

TARA PUBLISHING

Home Sweet Home

My family travel quite lot
They travel everywhere
'Wish you were here,' they write to me
But I'd rather not be there.

No me, I don't go anywhere
I like my cushioned chair.

They say it's nice to travel
To wander and to roam
But I feel that no matter what
There's no place quite like home.

Oh me, I don't go anywhere
I like the local air.

Why trudge across a desert
Why fly over a sea
When all my relatives can send
Their pictures home to me?

So me, I don't go anywhere
I prefer here to there.

Grandpa Laung at the Eiffel Tower

GRANDPA LAUNG

At The Eiffel Tower, Paris

Grandpa Laung has nimble toes
He dances wherever he goes
He danced along the Paris streets
He did a jig and tapped his feet.
He jigged right up the Eiffel Tower
But there he went too far –

The Eiffel Tower is very tall
My Grandpa Laung, he had a great fall.

Cousin Collum at the Tower Bridge

COUSIN COLLUM

At The Tower Bridge, London

Cousin Collum likes to measure
Everything in sight –
He measures them from up to down
And from left to right
He measures them from inside out
And by day and night
He measures them in colour and
Also in black and white.

He once measured the Tower Bridge
And secretly confessed
It was longer from the West to East
Than it was from East to West.

COUSIN PILLA

At The Leaning Tower, Pisa

Cousin Pilla's a fussy sort –
She went to Rome
And found it hot.

Venice made her fume and fret
Because she got
Her toenails wet.

At Pisa she was most irate
That they didn't set
The Tower straight.

She told them
'I don't want to wrangle
But I object to its acute angle.'

Cousin Pilla at the Leaning Tower

Uncle Tettra Hedran in a Great Pyramid

Uncle Tettra Hedran

In a Great Pyramid, Egypt

Uncle Tettra had four points to make

He made them clear and slow –

The first was

One

The second

Two

The third was

Eighty–four.

'The fourth – '

He said and then he stopped

And never spoke a word

He now lives in a pyramid

In Egypt, so we heard.

BROTHER MARBEL

At The Taj Mahal, India

My brother Marbel's rather slow
He likes to think things through
He ponders for an hour if you
Should ask him 'How are you?'

He sat before the Taj Mahal
For thirteen days and nights
And at the end he quietly said,
'This building's very white.'

Brother Marbel at the Taj Mahal

Great Aunt Kass Kade at the Victoria Falls

GREAT AUNT KASS KADE

At the Victoria Falls, Zimbabwe

My Great Aunt Kass Kade loves to wash
She likes to keep things clean
She washes up three times a day
And five times in between.

She scrubs and scrapes and brushes
And rinses everything
And when she's done, she starts again
Right from the beginning.

When she saw Victoria Falls
She cried, 'Oh, this is smashing!
If I had brought some soap along
I'd have done a whole month's washing!'

NEPHEW UNDAWATTAH

At the Great Barrier Reef, Australia

My nephew Undawattah

Is very, very shy.

When you ask him a question

He mumbles in reply.

He never does say hello

And he rarely says goodbye.

But at the Great Barrier Reef

When a shark swam by

He blushed a deep, tomato red

And suddenly shouted, 'Hi!'

Nephew Undawattah at the Great Barrier Reef

SISTER TAUCHBERRA

At The Statue of Liberty, New York

Tauchberra my little sister
Was born so small
We nearly missed her.

We took her home inside a cup
And used a spoon
To pick her up.

But after that
She grew and grew
And now no one
Can call her tiny

She went to New York
And she found
The top of Liberty's head
Was shiny.

Sister Tauchberra at the Statue of Liberty

Aunt Parapetta at the Great Wall

AUNT PARAPETTA

At The Great Wall, China

My maternal Aunt Parapetta
Wrote me a warm and touching letter
From China.

She wrote it in Chinese, so I couldn't see
What she wanted to say to me
From China.

I wrote her a reply, simple and plain –
'Could you write to me again
From China?'

She replied, this time in Cantonese
Except for the words 'my dear niece,
In China ...'

I gave up then and tried to call
But they said she'd gone to climb the Great Wall
Of China.

Brother-in-law Laa Vaa

At Mount Fuji-Yama, Japan

Laa Vaa, who's my brother-in-law
Is a weepy sort of bloke
He whimpers at a funny tale
And blubbers at a joke.

He went to see Fuji-Yama
He'd heard that it was nice
But when he saw the snow-capped peak
The tears came to his eyes.

He moaned and cried and bawled and wailed
When asked why he was weeping
He sobbed that it was sad to see
A volcano that's sleeping.

Brother-in-Law Laa Vaa at Mount Fuji-Yama

My Family

My family roams around the world
North, South, East and West
But when they're back they always say
That Home Sweet Home is best.

So me, I don't go anywhere
Why wander here and there?

© 2003 TARA PUBLISHING

Text:
Anushka Ravishankar

Illustrations:
Trotsky Marudu, Rathna Ramanathan,
T. Duraipandian and S.S. Ramani

Book Design:
Rathna Ramanathan, Minus 9 Design

Production:
C. Arumugam

Tara Publishing
38/GA, Shoreham
V Avenue, Besant Nagar
Chennai 600 090, India
E-mail: mail@tarabooks.com
www.tarabooks.com

ISBN: 81-86211-75-6